7536

Bus stop, bus go!

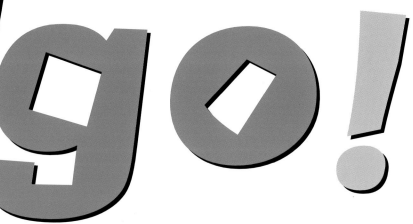

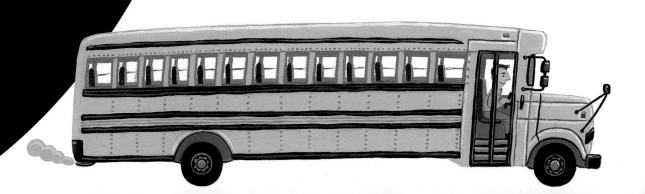

this book is for
Shannon, Hali, Casey,
Sophie, Lucy, Freddie,
Ivy, Raleigh, Russell,
and Maura

Copyright © 2001 by Daniel Kirk
All rights reserved. This book, or parts thereof,
may not be reproduced in any form without permission in writing from the publisher.
G. P. PUTNAM'S SONS,
a division of Penguin Putnam Books for Young Readers,
345 Hudson Street, New York, NY 10014.
G. P. Putnam's Sons, Reg. U.S. Pat. & Tm. Off. Published simultaneously in Canada.
Printed in Hong Kong by South China Printing Co. (1988) Ltd.
Book designed by Semadar Megged. Text set in AdLib.
The art was done in oil paint on gessoed paper.

Library of Congress Cataloging-in-Publication Data
Kirk, Daniel. Bus stop, bus go / Daniel Kirk. p. cm.
Summary: An escaped hamster enlivens the ride on an already chaotic school bus.
ISBN 0-399-23333-4
[1. School buses—Fiction. 2. Hamsters—Fiction. 3. Stories in rhyme.] I. Title.
PZ8.3.K6553 Bu 2001 [E]—dc21 00-040271
3 4 5 6 7 8 9 10

Bus stop, bus go!

Daniel Kirk

G. P. Putnam's Sons • New York

Bus stop, bus go!

Bus stop, bus go. See the children in a row.

Bus stop, bus go!

Hurry up, you play too slow.

Bus stop, bus go!

Brian, have you seen my—

No!

Bus stop, bus go!

All filled up to overflow.
At the schoolhouse, piling out,
children shove and children shout.